Thank you for becoming a friend
of Dew Bear and all the strange
and wonderful creatures of
Memory Forest and beyond.
We can't wait for you to
join us on this adventure.

Dew Bear

A Day in the Life of Dew

Saving Tessa

Book 3

Copyright © 2016 by Deborah Deel Clayton
A publication of Dew Bear Enterprises, Inc. - August 2016
Durham, NC, USA

Library of Congress Control Number 2016911745
ISBN 978-1-942261-08-7 (paperback)
ISBN 978-1-942261-09-4 (hardback)

For permission or comments, please e-mail the author, Deborah Deel Clayton, at dewbear@mindspring.com

Dew Bear strongly believes in giving back to the community. A portion of the net proceeds from the sale of every Dew Bear book will be donated annually to a specific charity. *The donation for Book 3 will go to Make a Wish Foundation.* Exact donation amounts will vary depending on associated costs to produce, publish, and sell the books.

A Day in the Life of Dew

Saving Tessa

Book 3

Written and illustrated by Deborah Deel Clayton
Published by Dew Bear Enterprises, Inc.
www.dewbear.com
email at dewbear@mindspring.com

No story would be complete without a cast of characters, whether it be a bear, a bird, a dragon, a loch ness monster, or any other potentially strange and wonderful creature. The Dew Bear series is filled with ever changing and new characters because that's how life is. Creatures come and go, while making their mark upon your life. I hope you will take the time to notice all the creatures that live in the illustrations of this book. Each picture can be a story in itself, and every creature portrayed has meaning in Dew's life.

This story was written with the help of Coral (my sister, Carol Tower). Hours spent on the phone evolved into a comical, thought provoking, and inspirational *Day in the Life of Dew*.

May every day in your life

be an adventure!

Dedicated to
Tessa Nault

A true life "Fabulous"
Character

Being unique is quite a talent !

TABLE OF CONTENTS

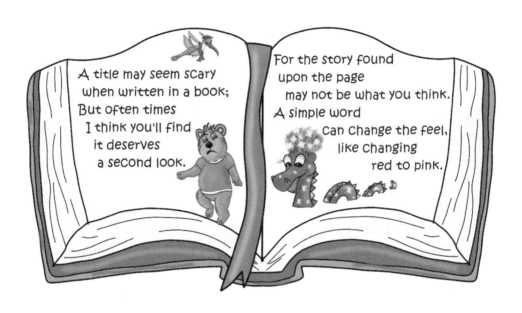

A title may seem scary
when written in a book;
But often times
I think you'll find
it deserves
a second look.

For the story found
upon the page
may not be what you think.
A simple word
can change the feel,
like changing
red to pink.

Prelude: The Life of Dew

Dew Bear was born
on a crisp autumn morn,
when dew on the grass was real thick.

Ma and Pa Bear
chose his name with great care,
'cause they knew
it was a name that would stick.

As Dew Bear grew,
everyone knew
they could count on him through and through;
For Dew Bear could do,
WHATEVER he put his mind to.

But Dew Bear knew,
he could count on his
family and friends too!

Once upon a time...

there was a very special monster who lived in Hidden Lake, just north of Peppermint Patty Park. Her name was Tessa.

Almost everyone, including Dew Bear, is scared of monsters, for they are the stuff of nightmares.

Tessa was different.

Thanks to her and a few hot days of summer, Dew Bear and his friends learned the value of not judging someone by what you think they might be, but rather by who they turn out to be.

Chapter 1 - The Day Begins

The last night of July slipped away, and the first dawn of August took its place. The morning started just as you'd expect from the last full month of Summer—hot and humid.

Dew's window remained open through the night, hoping to catch even the slightest breeze. His ceiling fan worked overtime, circulating the hot, sticky air throughout his bedroom. When Dew's eyes opened to the morning light, he found himself soaked in sweat.

That didn't bother Dew. He loved the heat. Summer was his favorite time of year because the days were filled with fun things

— like swimming in Soggy Boggy Bay, eating homemade ice cream at Penguin Palace, and having picnics with his friends. Today was just such a day.

Dew hopped out of bed before the sun rose in the gap between the mountains. He brushed his teeth, combed his fur, and changed into a green t-shirt and his favorite yellow swim trunks with palm trees all over them.

In the kitchen, Dew hummed a little tune as he retrieved his picnic basket from under

the counter. When he opened the lid, he found Holly, a small gray mouse, sleeping on the picnic tablecloth.

Dew whispered, "Holly, wake up. I need my basket today."

Holly opened her pretty yellow eyes, stretched her tiny legs, yawned, and slowly climbed out of the basket onto the counter.

"Sorry, Holly. I know it's early, but I'm meeting Sharky for a morning swim. Then we're having a picnic with Coral and Doeena," Dew said, placing some bananas, apples, and peaches in the basket.

He grabbed a big jar of sun tea from the fridge. **"Would you like to join us?"** Dew asked, placing the tea on the counter.

Holly shook her head no and in a very tiny voice said, **"I don't know how to swim."**

"I can teach you if you like," Dew said.

"Perhaps another day," Holly said. **"I think I'd rather sleep in this morning."**

Dew got a piece of bread out of the drawer and smeared a bit of honey on it. **"Here, you go, Holly. My apologies for having to wake you."**

Holly gratefully nibbled the bread and waved good-bye to Dew as he headed out the door.

Yes, this was going to be a fun summer day. Little did Dew know that other events were going on that would make this day—and the next couple days—even more fun.

Chapter 2 - Same Time Elsewhere

The early morning sun cast colorful hues across the water of Hidden Lake, like an artist with a paintbrush and a palette of pastels—pale yellow, soft pink, and warm blue. The colors danced across the water changing shapes. They blurred with the rise and fall of tiny waves created by Tessa's wake as she crisscrossed around the lake.

Tessa changed color to match the shifting waters.

Tessa was a Loch Ness Monster. She was not your ordinary monster; not by a long shot. She was an amazing monster by monster standards.

Tessa was quite unique. She had the ability to change her appearance anytime she wished. She  simply had to think **green** with **pink** polka dots and **yellow** braids, and she would be **green** with **pink** polka dots and **yellow** braids.

 If she thought **purple** with **green** stripes and **pink** horns, then she would turn **purple** with **green** stripes and **pink** horns.

She was very creative with her style choices and became known all over the lake as Tessa, the Fabulous Loch Ness Monster.

Tessa started out enjoying the colorful start of her day, chasing colors around the lake and reflecting that color in her scales. She changed colors so fast that someone watching the lake wouldn't see her. She became the same color as the water around her. The only thing that gave her away was the ripple of waves trailing behind her.

As the sun rose higher, and the sky took on a solid blue, Tessa once more changed to match the reflection in the water.

"Blue is my true color today," she said to the wind as it swirled around her, tickling her spines.

"Whhhhhhhhhyyyyyyy?" the wind asked as it dipped and rose and dipped again.

"My 10th birthday is in a couple days. Nobody has said anything about having a party," she said.

The wind moaned softly as it weaved in-between the spines on her back. It made Tessa laugh, and she changed to **pink** and covered herself in yellow flowers, including her hair.

"Have you heard any rumblings of a party?" Tessa asked, trying to visualize a cake and presents just below the water's surface.

"Noooooooooooooooooo," the wind whistled as it messed up her flowery hair.

"That's what I thought," Tessa said, disappointed. "I only turn 10 once!" she called out as the wind took to the sky to follow Sammy the seagull—leaving Tessa to the stillness of the hot, humid morning.

Chapter 3 - Visitors

As the day progressed, Tessa's color turned a darker shade of **blue**. She had swum around the lake twice already, wondering how to ask her friends if they were throwing her a surprise party. Suddenly, two little birds landed on her humps.

She immediately changed color to a soft **pink** with light **blue** hearts. Tessa loved company, and it showed.

"Hello!" said one of the birds. "I'm **Buddy, and this is Birdie.**"

"**It's nice to meet you,**" Tessa said. "**I've never seen you before. Do you live around here?**"

"We live at the southernmost point of Memory Forest, in the tree at Dew Bear's Den," Buddy tweeted.

"I swam down Black Brook as far as Soggy Boggy Bay one time," Tessa said.

"That must have been before the Beavers built the dam," Birdie chirped. "I don't think you could get past the dam now."

"Probably not," Tessa said. "So, what brings you to Hidden Lake?" she asked.

"We were visiting our mom who doesn't live far from here. We were asked to give you a message," Buddy said.

"Are you going to tell me about the birthday party?" Tessa asked, relieved that she would finally hear about her party.

"What birthday party?" Birdie asked.

"My party," Tessa said.

"When is it? Buddy asked.

"I thought you were going to tell me," Tessa said, showing her confusion by changing to **orange** with **green** question marks.

"We don't know anything about a birthday party," Birdie chirped. "But we love parties. We'd be happy to come to yours."

"If you don't have a message about my birthday party, then what message do you have for me?" Tessa asked.

"Our message is from your cousin, Fig," Buddy said.

"I didn't know I have a cousin named Fig," Tessa said, turning around and heading back towards Spirit Island.

"I think you knew him as Little One. He lived in Grundgy Meadow with Lissard and Groberjeff. He just moved into Dragon Hill, and now he goes by Fig," Birdie said.

"Oh, I know who you're talking about. So, is he throwing me a birthday party?" Tessa asked, thinking how wonderful that would be and turning a shade of yellow-green with **pink** hearts.

"He didn't say anything about your birthday or a party," Buddy chirped.

"Well, what *did* Fig say?" Tessa asked, growing frustrated with the conversation. Her color changed to **gray** with upside down marks that looked sorta like frowns—because that's how Tessa was feeling.

"He wants to know if you'd like to visit him," Buddy said.

"I think he wants to introduce you to some of his new friends," Birdie added.

"Hmmm..." Tessa thought for a minute. Her color changed to **purple**, a color half-way between happy and sad. "Tell Fig I'll come on Saturday. That's my birthday, but it doesn't seem like anyone around here is going to throw me a party. I might as well go enjoy myself."

"I have to say," Birdie tweeted, "our mom said you could change your appearance anytime you want, but I didn't believe her. Now that I've seen you do it a bunch of times, it really is amazing."

"**Thank you**," Tessa said, feeling proud.
She nodded her head good-bye.

As Buddy and Birdie circled back around
Hidden Lake to catch a strong wind current,
they watched Tessa change color to **green**.
Her scales were in the shape of **red** hearts, and
she had long **red**-**green** hair trailing behind
her as she hurried home.

Chapter 4 - An Idea

Buddy and Birdie found Fig sitting in the gnarly tree watching the Maxx & Jaxx rematch. It was a big event, and there was a good crowd cheering for Jaxx who was at bat.

Kelly Kat gave the fastball signal to Maxx as he wound up for the pitch.

"Strrrrriiiiike three!" hollered Kayla the giraffe as Jaxx swung and missed.

"That's three outs!" Triple T the beaver said. He was standing on the fence hoping to catch a foul ball in his baseball mitt.

"You were robbed," tweeted Neil the young cardinal as Jaxx tossed the bat down and headed to the pitcher's mound.

"You're back quick," Fig said to Buddy.

"We had a good tailwind coming back," Buddy said.

"So, will Tessa come visit me?" Fig asked.

"She will come in two days—on Saturday," Birdie chirped. "Did you know that day is Tessa's 10th birthday?" she asked.

"No, I didn't," Fig said.

"I think she was hoping her friends at Hidden Lake were going to throw her a birthday party," Buddy said. "She seemed very disappointed when our message wasn't about a party for her."

"Really? I've never thrown a party before, but perhaps I could give her a surprise party," Fig said. "Do you know how to plan a party? Who should I invite?" he asked.

"We've never thrown a party either, but we've been to lots of parties that Dew and his family have thrown. Maybe you could ask Dew for help," Birdie said.

"That's a wonderful idea," Alicia the bat said in a sleepy voice. She was hanging from a branch above Fig's head, trying hard to stay awake long enough to watch the game.

"I'll go find Dew as soon as the game is over. It's top of the 9th now," Fig said.

"What's the score?" Buddy asked.

"Tied up, but Jaxx gets to hit last," Fig said.

"We're hoping for an upset," Neil the cardinal chimed in. "Then there would be a re-match of the re-match."

"We'd love to stay and watch, but we've got to get home," Birdie tweeted as she took to the sky and tipped her wing in a wave. Buddy shrugged and took off after her.

The game ended with Jaxx hitting the winning run. After a few minutes of celebrating, almost everyone cleared out. That's when it dawned on Fig ... "Oh no! I forgot to ask Buddy and Birdie how to get to Dew's house."

Young Neil was still hanging around, playing tag with Julianna the dragonfly. He overheard Fig and said, **"Everyone knows where Dew lives. He's at the very end of the southernmost path. If you get lost, just ask anyone you meet along the way."**

"Thanks," Fig said. He took to the sky, heading south.

Sure enough, Fig found Dew's Den without any trouble. He knocked and knocked and knocked but got no answer. He was just about to fly back home when an alligator walked by.

"Are you looking for Dew?" the gator asked.

"I am," Fig said. "Is this his house?"

The gator eyed Fig a little suspiciously. She had never seen Fig before, but she knew that Dew had gone hunting a ferocious fire-breathing dragon a few weeks ago. She hadn't heard whether he found that dragon or not. Perhaps this was him. She was not going to give out information on Dew's whereabouts if this was a ferocious dragon.

Fig saw the distrust forming in the gator's eyes. He spoke up quickly. "I met Dew a couple weeks ago when I moved to Dragon Hill. My name is Fig."

"Are you the fierce fire-breathing dragon he went searching for?" she asked.

Stepping off the porch, Fig said, "I am the dragon he found, but I'm not really what he was searching for. I'm not very fierce, and I can't breathe fire. Dew and Kelly Kat were my first friends in Memory Forest ... besides Alicia the bat and her family."

"You know Kelly Kat and Alicia?" the gator asked.

"Yes, I do. Are they friends of yours?" Fig asked.

"Yes, they are. I've been away visiting family, so I guess I just haven't heard about you yet. Well, it's been nice talking to you, Fig, but I've got to get back home now," the gator said as she started walking away.

"Hey, what's your name?" Fig called after her.

"It's Ali-Gator," she said.

"Do you know where Dew is, Ali?" Fig asked.

"I just saw him and Sharky over at Coral's nest and Doe-ena's thicket," Ali called over her shoulder.

Fig took to the sky, thinking he knew where Coral's nest and Doe-ena's thicket was. It didn't take long for him to realize he was lost.

Chapter 5 - Lost

Fig landed on a branch in an old Oak tree. He knew right away it wasn't the tree he was looking for, but he had been flying around in circles and needed to get his bearings.

"**WHOoo ... are you?**" came a sweet voice out of the knot in the tree.

"**I'm Fig,**" Fig answered—not really sure who he was talking to.

"**WHOoo ... are you looking for?**" the voice asked.

"**Dew Bear,**" Fig replied. Out flew a magnificent barn owl with perfect shades of tan and white and the prettiest owl eyes.

"WHOoo ... you seek is straight ahead," the owl said, landing on the branch next to Fig.

"And 'WHOoo' are you?" Fig asked, playfully mimicking the Owl.

"WHOoo ... I am, is WHOoo ... I will be," the Owl said, smiling. Then she added, "I live in this tree—that's WHOoo ... I am!"

Fig liked her immediately. She was funny and charming at the same time. **"Can I ask your name?"** Fig asked.

The barn owl smiled shyly and said, **"My name is Who-rika."**

"Well, Who-rika, it has been my pleasure meeting you, and I hope to run into you again," Fig said. "But I must hurry and catch up with Dew Bear. I need to throw a surprise party for my cousin—but I have no idea how to plan one."

"Dew bear is WHOoo ... you need for that," Who-rika said, pointing towards Coral's tree.

Following her direction, Fig could barely make out Dew Bear and Sharky sitting on the ground in front of a white birch tree.

"Thanks for your help, Who-rika. Can I invite you to the party?" Fig asked.

"I would be happy to attend. WHOoo ... else will you be inviting?" she asked.

"All of Memory Forest," Fig said, waving good-bye and hurrying off towards Coral's tree.

Chapter 6 - Party Planning

Fig finally found Dew Bear. He was just sitting down to a picnic lunch. Fig landed at the edge of the picnic blanket.

"What a pleasant surprise," Dew said, shaking Fig's claw.

"Fig!" Sharky exclaimed, giving him a hug. **"So good to see you again. Would you like some tea and fruit?"**

"I'd love some," Fig said, taking an apple and a peach. **"I really came to ask a favor."**

Fig nodded his head at the beautiful white spotted deer standing behind Sharky. He smiled at the elegant green and yellow hummingbird who flew over his head.

"Hello, Fig, I'm Coral," the hummingbird said. She wore a pink scarf. It was swaying in the breeze created by the speed of her flapping wings. She had a matching hat with a blue feather.

"Yes," Dew said, "and this is Doe-ena."

Doe-ena bowed slightly and smiled at Fig. "Dew was just telling us about his dragon quest, and how he found you. I'm so glad you're not a fire-breather."

"Me too!" Fig said. "If I had been, I don't think we'd be having this conversation right now. Dew would have chased me away."

"That's right," Dew said. "So, what favor did you have in mind?"

"I've invited my cousin, Tessa, the Loch Ness Monster, for a visit Saturday. I just found out it's her 10th birthday. I'd like to throw her a surprise party, but I have no idea how to do that. Can you help me plan a party for her?" Fig asked.

"A party is a wonderful idea!!!" Dew said. "We all love parties, don't we?"

Sharky started dancing around, a huge grin on her face, spilling half her tea as she said, **"Perhaps we could have it at Peppermint Patty Park. It's such a great place for a party."**

"Since it's right off Potato Chip Creek," Doeena said, "Tessa won't have a problem getting there."

"I'm sure my family would love to host Tessa's party," Dew said, "and I'll bet Beezy will give us lots of honey," he added, putting the picnic basket in the wagon and scooping up a paw full of honey from the honey pot.

"I have leftover balloons from my birthday party," Doe-ena said.

"Could we invite everyone in Memory Forest?" Fig asked.

"Of course," Dew said. "Then everyone can meet you and your cousin too!"

"I can't wait to meet your cousin," Coral said. "I've never met a real live monster before."

All of a sudden, Dew Bear's face went white as a ghost. "M-M-Monster? I'm afraid of monsters!"

Fig put his arm around his friend and said, "Monster is just a title like Bear is to Dew Bear. A title doesn't make you who you are! Tessa's  not a scary monster. In fact, she's known as the Fabulous Loch Ness Monster. How can FABULOUS be scary?"

"I get it," Dew laughed. "It's like when I went dragon hunting thinking that all dragons were ferocious creatures. Then I found you!"

"Absolutely!" Fig said. "And now we are friends."

With that, they all put their heads together and started planning the surprise birthday party.

They drew up amazing invitations and enlisted the help of Buddy and Birdie to deliver them to everyone in Memory Forest. Fig made sure to include Ali-Gator and Who-rika.

You're Invited

Please join us for a Surprise Birthday Party on August 3rd at Peppermint Patty Park 2:00 pm to whenever Guest of Honor: Tessa (the Fabulous Loch Ness Monster)

Once the invitations were on their way, Fig, Coral, Doe-ena, Sharky, and Dew got to work ironing out the party details. Before the

sun went down, they had a complete list of all the things they would need and had figured out who would be responsible for each item.

"I'll come by in the morning with my wagon to pick up what you have ready," Dew said to Coral and Doe-ena. "Then I'll take it to Troll's bridge. I'm sure Troll won't mind giving me a ride in the Troll-ey car to deliver it all to Peppermint Patty Park.

"I'll meet you at Troll's bridge," Sharky said. "I'd love to help decorate."

"The more the merrier," Fig said. "We only have one day to get it all done, and I want it to be perfect." Fig took to the sky and headed home as a quarter moon was rising. It looked like a sideways smile in the sky—which was the perfect expression for how Fig was feeling.

Fig waved down to his friends, "Thanks for all your help. See you tomorrow."

Alicia the bat and her siblings caught up to Fig as he headed home. "We heard there's going to be a party on Saturday. What can we do to help?"

Fig filled Alicia in on all the plans as they made their way back to Dragon Hill, which was now growing into Memory Mountain.

Chapter 7 - Gathering Party Items

Dew arrived at Coral and Doe-ena's early the next morning, pulling his little blue wagon. He had already stopped at Beezy's and loaded up three honey pots.

"Morning ladies," Dew said.

"Morning, Dew," Coral said.

"It's a fine day for decorating," Doe-ena added. "I blew up some balloons, but there are lots more in the jar."

"I found some leftover birthday hats and candles," Coral said.

"I like this hat," Dew said, placing a purple one with streamers on his head.

"These are great party items," Dew said, tying the balloons to the wagon so they wouldn't fly away. He loaded the jar of extra balloons while Coral placed the party hats in the wagon. Dew held onto the candles so he wouldn't lose them. **"I'll meet you at Peppermint Patty Park,"** he said, pulling his loaded cart down the path towards Troll's Bridge.

"We'll be there right after we go see Pete and Peggy Penguin. We need to get them on board for making the ice cream," Coral called after him.

"Yes, ice cream is very important for a surprise party!" Dew hollered back before he turned the corner by Kelly Kat's Kave.

Kelly Kat was sharpening her claws on the trunk of a nearby tree when she saw Dew passing by.

"Hey, Dew," she called out.

"Hi, Kelly Kat," Dew said.

"I heard about the party for Fig's cousin. Can I help you decorate?" she asked, jumping down from the fence.

"Sure," Dew said. "We can use all the help we can get."

"Do you think Alicia and her bat family will be at the party?" Kelly asked.

"I wouldn't doubt it," Dew said. "Everyone in Memory Forest has been invited."

"Great," Kelly said. "I hope we get to play hide-n-seek at the party. Alicia is really good at that game. What are you giving Tessa as a gift?" she asked.

"I hadn't thought about it," Dew said.

"I'm giving her a really shiny piece of foil I found. It might have come off your cardboard sword the day of the dragon quest," Kelly said.

"That's pretty special, considering how much you like shiny things," Dew said.

"I thought about keeping it for myself, but I know you're always saying it's better to share," she said.

"Yes, it is," Dew said. "I'm sure Tessa will appreciate your thoughtful gift."

"If she doesn't, she can give it back to me on my birthday!" Kelly said with a grin.

They arrived at Troll's Bridge just as Sharky was coming up the path from Soggy Boggy Bay. She was having a hard time carrying all the stuff she had, and something fell on the ground.

"I'll get it," Kelly called out. She raced over to Sharky and grabbed the gift bag in her mouth.

"Thanks, Kelly," Sharky said. "I should have borrowed Dew's wagon."

Troll was waiting for them, wiping some paw prints off the hood of his car.

"That wasn't me," Kelly said to Troll.

"I can tell," Troll said. "These are much bigger paws—more like Jocelynn's size!"

Jocelynn the jaguar was on a branch of the nearby oak tree. "The hood of your car is nice and warm," she hollered down to Troll.

"Next time, just wipe your paws before you jump up," Troll hollered back.

"I'll try to remember," Jocelynn said.

"Are you going to the party tomorrow?" Kelly Kat hollered up to her.

"Wouldn't miss it," Jocelynn said. She yawned and laid her head on her paws. It was time for a cat-nap.

There was so much party stuff, all of it wouldn't fit in the trunk. Troll had to tie the lid down with a strap. "We better get a move on," he said. They piled into the car and took off to pick-up Fig.

As they drove along Potato Chip Creek, it seemed that everyone had heard about the party and was on their way to Peppermint Patty Park to help decorate.

Chapter 8 - Decorating

Fig was waiting for them as they rounded the bend by Memory Mountain. When Fig first moved in, the mountain was nothing more than a mound of dirt, known as Dragon Hill. But now, every time Fig thinks of something good in his life, a memory stone gets added, and the hill grows.

"This party will add lots of memory stones to your mountain," Sharky said.

"Yesterday's party planning stone popped up this morning. It's on the left corner, over the entrance," Fig said.

"You'll have to ride on the hood," Troll said. "There's no room in the back seat."

"Wow, that sure is a lot of stuff," Fig said, climbing onto the hood. "Planning a party is lots of fun."

"Can't wait for tomorrow!" Toucan Tom hollered down as he flew overhead. He had a present in his claws.

It didn't take long to reach Peppermint Patty Park, even though Troll had to drive real slow so Fig wouldn't fall off.

As they drove down the long dirt driveway, Fig said, "I don't want to put up the banner until tomorrow. I was thinking that I'd meet Tessa at my place, then tell her I want to introduce her to a few friends. We'll come back up this way. You guys can hang the banner where she'll see it and then yell ... SURPRISE!"

"That will be so cool," Sharky said.

"I like that idea," Troll said. "Since Lankey, Jambo, and I are the tallest, we can handle that. We can hang it between a couple trees near the creek entrance."

"Perfect," Fig said, carrying the jar of balloons over to Lankey. He and Marzipan had the job of blowing them up.

"Bout time you got here," Ma said. "Critters have been showing up all morning asking to help. I got them started, but I've got to get back to baking the cake!"

"Thanks, Ma," Dew said, helping Troll unload the trunk.

"Wow, what great stuff," Connie Sue said, peeking in Sharky's box.

I know just where these fish hangers can go," Honey Bear said. She and Carolina grabbed the fish and headed for the porch.

Sharky and Kelly Kat went in the house to help Ma Bear bake the birthday cake. **"I call the frosting spoon,"** Sharky said, closing the door behind her.

Doe-ena and Coral showed up in no time. **"Pete and Peggy Penguin are working on homemade ice cream. They'll have it ready by morning,"** Coral said.

"Sounds delicious," Troll said. **I hope they make chocolate. That's my favorite."**

Doe-ena helped Connie Sue and Norma Jean twist the colorful streamers. Coral helped the birds put the streamers in place.

There was lots of laughter, and by the end of the day, they had the whole place looking festive.

"I can't thank you all enough for helping me with this party," Fig said as everyone started leaving. "I'll see you tomorrow."

"Happy to help," Ma Bear said.

"We love parties," Pa Bear said, grabbing his guitar. "I better get this in tune so it'll be ready for tomorrow." He started strumming a song. Before long, Dew's brothers, Lankey and Bubbly, picked up their banjos and started playing. Marzipan used his spoons to tap out the beat on the old wash tub. Dook drank the rest of the honey juice and blew into the jug, creating a deep back-beat to the song.

They were practicing the 'Happy Birthday' song when Dew, Fig, Sharky, Kelly Kat, and Troll headed for home.

Chapter 9 - Tessa's Journey

On Saturday, August 3rd, Tessa woke as the sun was just peaking over the horizon. She was anxious to get going but couldn't make up her mind what color to be.

Gloria the goldfish was swimming nearby. **"Hey, Gloria,"** Tessa called out.

Gloria poked her head out of the water. **"Morning, Tessa,"** she said.

"I'm going to visit my cousin today. Can you help me decide which color I should be?" Tessa asked.

"Sure," Gloria said. **"What are you thinking?"**

"Well, I'm excited, so I was thinking maybe bright **pink** with some yellow. How does this look?" Tessa asked, changing color to be bright **pink** with yellow curly cues and spines.

"Spectacular as always," Gloria said.

"Whatcha up to?" asked Patricia the parrot fish, poking her head out of the water.

"Tessa's going on a trip and wants to know what color looks best on her," Gloria said.

"What else you got?" Patricia asked.

"I'm a bit nervous. How about green with a splash of **rainbow**." She changed color to two shades of green with **rainbow** colored hair and spines. She added a yellow bow at the end of her long fluffy hair.

"That's cool too," Gloria said.

"I like both combinations," came a voice behind Tessa. She turned to see Shelly the sea turtle floating on top of the water.

"Well, I can do green with pink polka dots, yellow hair, and rainbow spines," she said proudly, changing colors.

"That's the one," Gloria said.

"Breathtaking," Patricia said.

"Perfect," Shelly said.

Tessa looked over her shoulder at the sun. It was climbing higher in the sky, and clouds were forming over the mountains.

"I better get going. Thanks for your help," Tessa said, nodding good-bye to her friends and heading towards the entrance to Potato Chip Creek.

Unlike her cousin Fig, she did not have wings to fly. She had to travel by water. But that was not a problem because Potato Chip Creek, which ran through Memory Forest, started at Hidden Lake. All she had to do was follow the creek until she got to Dragon Hill. That shouldn't be a problem at all.

As Tessa made her way through the narrow opening, she realized that not one of her friends wished her a happy birthday. "I guess no one remembered my special day," she said to herself as she picked up speed, putting some distance between her and Hidden Lake.

Susie the butterfly was flying overhead when she heard Tessa's comment. She hurried over to Gloria, Patricia, and Shelly who had now been joined by Ray the stingray and Sammy the seagull. They were talking quietly.

"Do you think she suspects anything?" Shelly asked.

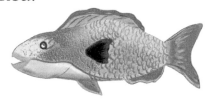

"I don't think so," Patricia said.

"Tessa's not good at hiding her emotions," Gloria said. "If she knew about

a party, she would have turned a happy color and covered herself in presents and birthday hats."

"I think you're right," Susie said, joining the conversation. "I just heard her say that no one remembered her special day."

"Let's give her a few minutes to get well ahead of us. Then we'll head on  down to Peppermint Patty Park," Ray said.

"I can't wait to see her face when she sees all of us there," Sammy said, heading back to his nest to get Tessa's present.

Meanwhile, Tessa made great time until she got to the stone bridge near Peppermint Patty Park. It had a low clearance and was dark—two things Tessa did not like.

She squinted into the dark opening, held her breath, and changed color to **gray** to blend with the darkness. She added **pink** and **purple** hair with a few strands of glow to light the way.

Just as she dipped her head down to enter the tunnel, a soft voice from under the bridge said, **"Hello."**

Tessa stopped just short of going into the darkness. **"Who's there?"** she called out.

"Just me," Ma Troll said, stepping into the light.

Ma Troll was a short, pudgy troll with pretty green eyes. She was wearing a purple dress with matching hat and was holding a bouquet of yellow flowers. She was nothing like what Tessa imagined a Troll would look like. Tessa changed color to **purple** to match Ma Troll's dress. She covered herself in spots shaped like yellow flowers.

"How pretty," Ma Troll said. **"I was just fixing brunch. Would you like to join me?"**

Tessa's tummy rumbled. "I guess the answer is yes," she said. "I was so anxious to get on my journey, I forgot to eat breakfast."

"Wonderful, dear," Ma Troll said. She led Tessa under her bridge. Once Tessa's eyes adjusted to the dim light, she could see Ma Troll had a very nice spot under the bridge.

"Here you go, my dear," Ma Troll said, passing Tessa a plate of seaweed salad and a cup of fresh-made lemonade.

"So, what brings you down Potato Chip Creek?" Ma Troll asked.

"I'm on my way to visit my cousin, Fig. He lives at Dragon Hill. Do you know where that is?" Tessa asked.

"It's just past Peppermint Patty Park, around the bend past the weeping willow tree ... but, we won't be calling it Dragon Hill for long," she said. "It's growing into a mountain now. You can't miss it, my dear."

Tessa finished her seaweed salad and let out a tiny burp. "Oh, excuse me," she said.

"That's okay, deary. I always say there's more room outside than in," Ma Troll laughed.

"Thank you for a wonderful lunch and great company," Tessa said. She kissed Ma Troll on the cheek and headed on her way down Potato Chip Creek.

Chapter 10 - Stuck in the Muck

As Tessa passed Peppermint Patty Park, she could hear music. Tessa loved music. **"Someone must be having a party,"** she said to the gust of wind that whipped around her head. She tried peering through the trees, but they were too thick.

She noticed a tiny inlet leading away from Potato Chip Creek, towards the music. Tessa was tempted to take a detour. **"If I hadn't stopped for brunch, I could do it,"** she said to a butterfly fluttering past. The butterfly waved and flew into the woods.

"I better hurry along—I don't want to keep Fig waiting." As Tessa swam past the inlet opening, she started thinking about country music stars. She changed to a light **gray** with **colorful** stars.

The music was fading away as Tessa swam under the hanging branches of the willow tree that Ma Troll mentioned. They felt tickly as they glided over her humps. Tessa changed to the playful color of **teal** with **orange** tickle-feather hair. She giggled and startled a dragon lizard who was sunning herself on a nearby rock.

The lizard leaped off the rock and started running away down the shoreline. **"Hey, wait!"** Tessa said, swimming after her. **"I didn't mean to scare you."**

The lizard looked over her shoulder but kept on running.

Tessa swam as fast as she could, trying to catch up to the lizard. All of a sudden, the water level dropped. Tessa was high and dry. Not a good thing for a Loch Ness Monster.

"HEEEEELP!!!" Tessa cried out, struggling to free herself from the mucky sandbar.

"**What's the problem?**" asked a clown fish who happened to be snorkeling nearby.

"**I'm stuck!**" Tessa squealed, wiggling side to side. "**Can you help me get free?**"

"I'm too small to help you," the clown fish said, "but I'll go get my sister, Shayla. She's very smart 'cause she goes to fish school." The clown fish ducked under the water and started swimming downstream.

" Please, don't leave me here alone!" Tessa hollered after him.

"I'll be right back," he said. "If you need me sooner, just say my name in an air bubble under water. When it pops, I'll hear you and come back," the clown fish added as he started off again.

"Wait!" Tessa called after him. "What's your name?"

"Bryce!" shouted the clown fish as he swam away at top speed.

While Bryce was gone, Tessa squirmed and wiggled and stretched, trying to free herself from the mud. With every inch forward, she sank deeper in the muck. Soon, the mud was halfway up her humps, and she couldn't move at all.

"**I'm back,**" Bryce shouted as he popped his head out of the water a few feet away.

Shayla approached Tessa shyly. As Bryce said, she was smart—she knew to be cautious of strangers.

Tessa spoke first, "**Can you help me little koi fish? I think your name is Shayla, right?**"

"**That's right,**" Shayla said. "**But Daddy says not to talk to strangers.**"

"**I'm not really a stranger,**" Tessa said. "**I've come to visit my cousin, Fig. Do you know him?**"

"I do," Shayla said. "But how do I know that you are who you say you are?" she asked.

"She must be," Bryce said. "Why else would she be stuck in the muck?"

Shayla gave Bryce a koi look and said, "Bryce, when you go to school next year, you'll learn how to keep yourself safe. But, right now, I'm the big sister, so I have to protect us."

Tessa was getting frustrated, and that made her think of **gray**. We all know what happens when Tessa thinks a color ... Shayla watched Tessa change colors right before her eyes. One minute Tessa was **teal** with **orange** feathery hair. The next, she was **gray** with **purple** spines and **pink** hair. Then she threw on some bright **pink** diamonds to mimic Shayla's **pink** scales. To top it off, Tessa added a **gold** hoop earring.

"How did you do that?" Shayla asked.

"I just think it, and it happens," Tessa said.

"Wow! Can I do that too?" Bryce asked.

"I don't know," Tessa said. "I've found some creatures can and some can't. You just have to think real hard and see if it happens."

Bryce closed his eyes and thought and thought and thought about changing the colors of his stripes from **orange** to **blue**. When he opened his eyes, his stripes were still **orange**. He scrunched his eyes hard and thought with all his might. When he opened his eyes, there was no change in color.

"You're distracting me, Shayla," Bryce said.

"How am I distracting you? I'm not doing anything," Shayla said.

"You're watching me—I can feel it," Bryce said.

"Oh, brother," Shayla said, turning her back to Bryce. Shayla closed her eyes, saying **"I like purple and black."** When she opened her eyes, poof ... she was **purple** with **black** spots.

She tried it again, and poof ... she changed to **green** and **yellow**.

"Thanks for sharing your secret," Shayla said to Tessa.

"I'm happy to share," Tessa said, **"because sharing makes everyone happy."**

"No fair!" Bryce said. **"I'm trying real hard, but it's not working."** He thought harder and harder. When he opened his eyes, he still saw **orange** stripes.

Shayla started laughing and pointing at him. "**What?**" Bryce asked, looking at his fins. "I'm still **orange** and **white**."

"Yes, but your eyes changed from **blue** to **green**," Shayla said.

"**They did?**" Bryce asked, staring down into the water so he could see his reflection. "**They did!**" he said.

"**Look what I can do!**" Bryce shouted with glee, swimming over to a dragonfly and two butterflies hovering near shore.

"I'm glad you both can change color," Tessa said, "but I've really got to get out of this muck soon."

"We're not strong enough to get you out, but I know someone who can help," Shayla said.

"Dew Bear?" Bryce asked.

"Yep," Shayla said. "Dew Bear can do everything. I'm sure he can get you unstuck."

Tessa wiggled a little harder, but she was as stuck as stuck can be. "You better get him fast, or I may be permanently stuck here!"

"Bryce, you're the fastest swimmer, so go find Dew. I think he's visiting his mom in Peppermint Patty Park." Before Shayla could finish her words, Bryce was long gone.

"It shouldn't take long for Dew to get here," Shayla said.

"I wish I could swim as fast as Bryce right now," Tessa said, "then I could get myself out of this mucky situation." But, the closest she could come to being a clown fish was to change her appearance to look like one. She changed to **orange** and **white** stripes with **black** spines.

Changing appearance didn't get her out of the muck, but she felt better knowing help would soon arrive.

Chapter 11 - The Solution

Bryce was back in no time with Dew Bear running along the shoreline. He wasn't alone. Most everyone in Memory Forest came out to see what all the commotion was about.

Coral flew out and landed on one of Tessa's spines. Tessa was so pleased with all the help, she changed to **pink** and covered herself in **colorful** hearts. "Tessa, I'm Coral. **Fig told us you were coming to visit today. So sorry you got stuck in this muck. But, don't worry, Dew will figure this out.**"

Dew waded into the water. It got waist deep within a few feet. When Dew realized he wouldn't be able to walk out to Tessa, he turned around and headed back to shore.

Troll pulled up in the Troll-ey car a few minutes later with Sharky at his side.

"Sharky, can you swim out to Tessa and keep her calm? It's too deep for me to wade out there."

"Sure," Sharky said, diving in the water.

"Tell her we're working on a plan," Dew hollered after her.

Who-rika flew onto the nearby fence post, and Ali-gator swam up the creek.

"Ali," Dew said. "Did you see the Beavers on your way up the creek?"

"Nope. I don't know if they've left Beaver Dam yet," She said.

"Good," Dew said. "Who-rika, can you do me a favor? Fly over to Beaver Dam. Tell Brainiac and Triple-T that we need them right away."

"**Sure thing, Dew,**" Who-rika said, taking flight and out of sight in seconds.

Dew was pondering the situation when Ribbet the frog croaked, "**Can I help?**"

"**Actually, you can,**" Dew said. "**I need to know how long the sandbar is. You're really good in the muck—can you go check that out for me?**"

"I can get you out there quicker," Ali said to Ribbet, bending her snout to the water so he could climb on. Ali glided out to the sandbar ... it was a good excuse to go meet Tessa.

"Hello, Tessa," Ali said as Ribbet dove right in, taking measurements from front to back and side to side.

Ribbet needed to get the dimensions back to Dew quickly, but Ali was in the middle of a conversation with Tessa.

"Hey, Bryce, can you give me a ride back to shore?" Ribbet asked.

"Oh, yes," Bryce said. "I'm even faster than Ali. Hold on tight!"

Ribbet held onto Bryce's top fin as they sped towards shore.

"The sandbar is just a smidge longer and wider than Tessa," Ribbet told Dew.

"Great," Dew said. "That means we just need to raise the water level in that little bit of Potato Chip Creek."

Who-rika landed on the fence near Dew. "Beavers are on their way. They were just past Fish School when I caught up with them. They should be here any minute."

Dew turned around, and sure enough, Brainiac and Triple-T came jogging around the bend.

"What do you need us to do?" Brainiac asked.

"Tessa's stuck on that sandbar. It's not much longer or wider than she is, so I'm thinking ..."

"Build a dam!" Triple-T shouted.

"That's right," Dew said. "How quickly could you build one to raise the water level?"

"Lickety split!" Brainiac said. "Triple-T, swim to the other side of the creek and start cutting down trees. Dew, you organize some helpers to carry the wood over to me. We'll build it in that narrow part right there."

Triple-T got to work. They don't call him "Tabor Tooth Tyler" for nothing. He chewed through trees faster than a toothpick.

Ali-Gator led the team of helpers to carry the sticks and branches over to Brainiac, so he could place them just right.

With all that help, the dam was finished in no time.

"That does it," Brainiac said, placing the last branch in place. **"Won't take long now for the water to rise."**

Sure enough, within minutes, Tessa could feel the water climbing up her humps. Her tail came free of the muck. **"It's working,"** she shouted.

Everyone cheered as Tessa wiggled and squirmed and finally broke free of the mucky muck. She was so grateful to everyone for all their hard work getting her unstuck, she swam around the shore, down past the dam, and back up the other shore. **"Thank you so much,"** she said to everyone as she passed them by, turning a watery shade of **blue** with **pink** hearts.

When Tessa came to Dew Bear, she said, "Thank you, Dew, for figuring out how to get me unstuck." Then Tessa said sadly, "I was on my way to visit my cousin, Fig. I guess I won't get to see him now."

"Sure you will," Dew said. "He's not at Memory Mountain right now. He's back the way you came ... just upstream at my family's place in Peppermint Patty Park."

"He is?" Tessa asked. "Then why didn't he come with you to help get me unstuck?"

"He wanted to come, but he's helping my family with a little project," Dew said, winking at Troll.

"Follow us, and we'll take you to him," Sharky said.

Everyone headed back up Potato Chip Creek towards Peppermint Patty Park ... some by water, some by land.

During the short trip, Bryce and Shayla told everyone how Tessa taught them to change color. Shayla demonstrated by changing to a smooth body of yellow and purple with colorful spots. Everyone oohed and awed.

"Look what I can do," Bryce said closing his eyes and thinking hard. He thought about changing his eye color from green back to his normal blue. "Blue eyes .... blue eyes .... blue eyes!" he chanted.

When he opened his eyes for everyone to see, Shayla said, "Ah ... Bryce, your eyes are still green."

"Ah, man," he said. "I tried real hard."

Shayla was pointing at him and laughing. "What????" Bryce asked impatiently.

"Your eyes are still green, but one of your fins is blue."

Bryce looked at his fins — one was orange and one was blue. He closed his eyes again, and poof ... the other fin turned blue. "I think I got it now," he said. He closed his eyes one last time, thought real hard, and when he looked at his stripes ... they were blue, and so was his tail fin. "I did it!" he shouted, happier than he had ever been in his whole life. It didn't matter that his eyes were still green.

Tessa smiled at Bryce. "Sometimes it takes time to change. When I first started changing, my color schemes were all over the place. I had a hard time controlling them. But now I can change at will. I'm proud of you for sticking with it, Bryce."

Doe-ena was fascinated. She was secretly trying to change the color of her spots—but every time she looked, they were still **white**. Then she got an idea and said, "I can change the color of my spots."

"You can?" Bryce asked. "Do you have the secret power too?"

"Nope, I don't have a secret power," Doe-ena said. "But I can still change. Do you want to see?" she asked.

"Oh, yes!" Bryce said, excited to watch her change.

Doe-ena stepped over to the edge of the creek, laid down, and rolled over on her back. She shimmied a few times for good measure. When she stood up, her **white** spots were **brown**. "See?" Doe-ena said "Anyone can change if they really want to!"

Everyone laughed at the sight of Doe-ena covered in mud, but she made her point.

Chapter 12 - Let the Party Begin

"**We're here,**" Dew said, changing direction and heading down the little inlet that led to Peppermint Patty Park—the same one that Tessa spotted earlier.

"**I almost went down this waterway earlier. I heard music,**" Tessa said.

"**That was probably my family fooling around,**" Dew said.

"**They were very good,**" Tessa said. Then she caught sight of Fig waving to her from the bank that ran past an old shack.

There was a big banner between the trees with balloons. As she got closer, Tessa saw the words just as everyone shouted them ...

HAPPY BIRTHDAY TESSA

Tessa immediately turned an embarrassed shade of **red** with soft **green** hearts, **orange** spines, and matching **wild** hair. "What a wonderful surprise!" she said. "How did you know it was my birthday?"

"A couple birdies told us," Fig said, laughing as Buddy and Birdie landed on Tessa's humps.

"We're glad you made it, Tessa," Buddy chirped.

As Tessa glided along the shoreline, she saw the table with the tall cake and lots of presents. That made Tessa very happy. She changed to her favorite color, **teal**, with splashes of presents and birthday hats. She added **colorful** streamers to her head and changed her spines to look like balloons.

"**I told you,**" Gloria said to Ray and Patricia as they dove beneath the surface to breathe. "**Tessa can't hide her feelings.**"

"**It's her best one yet,**" Patricia laughed. "**I'd say she's ready for her party now!**"

All of Tessa's friends from Hidden Lake came, but there were many new faces too. Scanning the crowd, she recognized one. **"Ma Troll, did you know about this earlier?"**

"Yes, dear. But a surprise must remain a surprise right up to the end," Ma Troll said, giving Tessa her present and a hug.

Tessa had just taken a bite of rainbow cake and ice cream, when Liz the lizard introduced herself, **"Hello, Ms. Tessa."**

Tessa swallowed, enjoying the combination of flavors. She tasted vanilla mixed with oranges, strawberries, blueberries, grapes, and broccoli—which actually tasted pretty good in a cake. Tessa changed to look like her **rainbow** cake and covered herself in pinwheels, like the one that Liz was giving her as a present. **"You're the lizard from the rock near the weeping willow tree,"** Tessa said. **"I'm so sorry that I scared you. I didn't mean to run you off."**

"You didn't really scare me," Liz said. **"I ran because I figured you must be the**

Tessa everyone was talking about. I knew if you spoke to me, I'd blabber all about your surprise party. Anyone here will tell you that I can't keep a secret!"

"Well, I have a secret I'd be happy to tell you," Tessa said.

"Are you sure you want to do that? I'll probably tell everyone," Liz said.

Tessa nodded. "My secret is that this is the very best birthday party I've ever had!"

"I'll be happy to share that secret," Liz said, taking off to spread the word.

As daylight was changing to dusk, Jaxx, the little red squirrel, jumped up on the fence near Tessa. "I know a secret. Do you want to hear it?" he asked.

"Sure," Tessa said, leaning in close so Jaxx could whisper in her ear.

"This is the best party ever, and you love us all!" he said with an ear to ear grin.

"Well, that's not exactly what I said," Tessa laughed. "It's even better!"

"What do you mean?" Jaxx asked.

"I started the secret a couple hours ago," Tessa said.

"You did?" Jaxx asked.

Tessa nodded her head yes as Jaxx jumped down from the fence and ran over to his brother. "Hey, Maxx!" Jaxx said. "I know a secret about the secret."

Tessa's 10th birthday party was the biggest party Memory Forest had ever seen. Everyone was there, and they all got their chance to meet and talk to Tessa. Each one fell in love with her.

After hours of cake, ice cream, cookies, and lots of other delicious items—the likes of which Tessa had never tasted before—the party was coming to an end.

The quarter moon rose with an even brighter sideways smile than it had two evenings prior. By the light of the happy moon and a sky full of stars, Fig rounded everyone up for one final birthday toast. **"To my fabulous cousin,"** Fig began, **"a monster to which** no other can compare; with a gentle soul and a kind heart. Tessa, we hope your 10th birthday was as wonderful as you are!"

Tessa felt all warm and tingly, like she imagined a star would feel. She immediately turned a deep shade of **night** and let her stars shine through. It was a dazzling combination and a perfect way to end a perfect day.

Chapter 13 - One for Good Measure

As Dew climbed into bed, he realized that being afraid of monsters just because they're called monsters was foolish of him.

"I must have seemed like a monster when you first met me," Dew said to Holly who was standing on his nightstand.

She tilted her head, batted her sleepy eyelashes, and climbed down into the drawer that Dew left open for her. His soft t-shirts made a great place to sleep.

"You never know who you're going to meet on your journey through life," Dew said as he cut off the light. **"But if you open your heart, you just might become friends."**

Meanwhile, on the other side of Memory Forest, at the edge of Spirit Island, Tessa changed to her bedtime **gray** and covered herself in cuddly teddy bears. She stared up at the star filled night. **"I wished upon the brightest star and asked for a birthday party, but what I got was so much more,"** she said to the wind which was making its evening trip around the lake.

"The greatest gift I got today didn't come in a fancy bag or box. It wasn't tied up with pretty ribbons. Do you know what it was?" she asked.

"Noooooooooooo" the wind whispered.

Tessa yawned, closed her eyes, and said softly, **"It was love."**

The End

How much is a new adventure worth?

While Dew and Sharky enjoy a warm summer day at Soggy Boggy Bay, Sharky wants to know Dew's thoughts ... but he has to pay for them. A penny changes hands and starts on a journey through Memory Forest. Who will share in the penny's adventure, and where will it come to rest?

Join Dew and friends as they ponder the penny's purpose. We promise you'll never look at a penny the same way again!

Next up ...

A Day in the Life of Dew
Book 4
A Penny for Your Thoughts

"A Day in the Life of Dew" - Who's Who?   Page 1 - Family

Dew   Ma Bear   Pa Bear   Bubbly   Lankey

Marzipan   Dook   Jambo   Big Bob   Dunloper

Connie Sue   Norma Jean   Carolina   Honey Bear

"A Day in the Life of Dew" - Who's Who? Page 2 - Friends

Beezy Sharky Coral Doe-ena

Fig Who-rika Ali-Gator Buddie & Birdie

Troll Ma Troll Mot Krank Kelly Kat

Pete & Peggy Penguin Vicky Vulture Dude Vulture Grandpa Vulture

"A Day in the Life of Dew" - Who's Who?

Tessa   Brainiac   Triple "T"

Shayla   Bryce   Ribbet   Rebbit

Suzie   Julianna   Crystal Gail   Chelly

Elly   Mrs. Hawk   Louise   Mr. & Mrs. Fields

"A Day in the Life of Dew" - Who's Who?

Lissard   Groberjeff   Antoinette & Kiki

Mr. Pickle   Sarah   Margaret   Viper

Say   Fred   Shirl   Shadow

Dustin   Andy   Alex   Jay

"A Day in the Life of Dew" - Who's Who?

Katie

Jake

Jenny

Shelli

Sammy

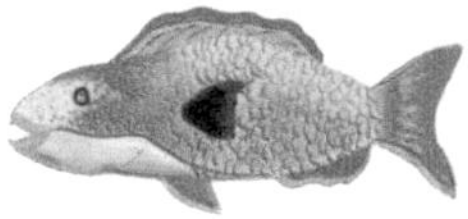

Patricia

Lakesha

Nancy

Gloria

Kris

Ray

Ian

Bobby
the Balding Eagle

"A Day in the Life of Dew" - Who's Who?   Page 6 - Friends

Holly   Ross   Ryan   Ricky   Kayla

Maxx & Jaxx   Terry   Alicia   Jocelynn

Derrek   Brandon   Tom   King Brian

Miss Jess   Dragon King   Chase   Shannon Bear

Colton   Mamacita   Theo   Red   Young Neil

127

Not all these characters are in this book –
some are in others.
And, some are missing, because Dew
has not met them yet. But, he is always
on the lookout for new friends
as he embarks on new adventures!

So, collect all of Dew Bear's adventures
and become friends with all the
strange and wonderful creatures of
Memory Forest and beyond!!!

"Life is just a journey,
a long and winding road;
And everyone along the way,
is someone you get to know!"

Dew Bear

Dew Bear is scared of Monsters ...
until Fig explains that Monster is just a title,
like Bear is to Dew Bear.

Tessa is a Fabulous Loch Ness Monster
If you could be like her,
what colors would you be?

If Bryce thinks and thinks and thinks ...
what color will he be?

Shayla can change
many colors.
What color is she
thinking now?

Start

Finish

Dew is scared of monsters. But if he finds his way to Tessa, he'll learn that some monsters are really worth knowing!!!

Can Tessa make it down Potato Chip Creek without getting stuck on a sandbar?

If she gets stuck, Dew & Friends will figure out a way to save her.

Dew sends Who-rika to find the beavers, Brainiac & Triple T.

Can you help her find her way to Beaver Dam?

Watch for these and other stories
so you can continue the Adventure of

A Day in the Life of Dew

Book 1 - Dew has a M.O.M. (Mountain of Memories)

Follow Dew's adventure as he makes his way to Peppermint Patty Park to visit his Mom on Mother's Day. Join the celebration, and meet the strange and wonderful creatures who live in Memory Forest, in this first book of the series.

Book 2 - Dragon Quest

Dew dreams of ferocious Dragons, and the next day, sets out on an adventure to protect Memory Forest from the last Dragon—that is, till he meets Fig. Join Dew on his quest and make a lasting friend.

Book 3 - Saving Tessa

Fig's cousin Tessa is turning 10. Join everyone in Memory Forest for her birthday celebration in Peppermint Patty Park. But first, Dew must find a solution to a very mucky situation.

Book 4 - A Penny for Your Thoughts (Winter 2016)

Join Dew Bear and Sharky for some ice cream, and follow a penny's journey, as it makes its way from Soggy Boggy Bay to Penguin Palace.

Other stories – order of release undetermined

Sharky's Special Day

When Dew finds out that Sharky doesn't have a birthday, he gets together with his friends and plans a very special day indeed!! Find out how Sharky ended up in Soggy Boggy Bay.

A Hero in Memory Forest

Dew and his friends are in a drought, and there's little food to be found. Find out who saves the day in a very special way.

Trick-or-Treat'ment'

Join Dew and friends as they dress up for Halloween. Walk the Haunted Trail and bob for apples at the Hallow-scream party. But, there's a reason you shouldn't eat the whole bag of candy at one time!!!

Small Can be Just the Right Size

Join Dew and friends for a game of golf that turns into a rescue mission ... or does it? Sometimes things are not always the way they seem.

A Honey of a New Friend

Take a journey back in time and learn how Dew met his good friend Beezy.

Troll's Birthday Celebration

(and Dew gets a Tummy Ache)

Join Dew and friends for Troll's Birthday Celebration. But, don't eat too much cake, or you too will have to visit Dr. Rosati for help with a tummy ache.

A Ghostly Adventure

Join Dew and friends as they go camping in Memory Forest. But watch out for those Ghost Stories around the campfire!!!

Home is Where the Heart Is!

Fig finally finds his parents. Will he leave Memory Forest and join them in the far away Enchanted Everglades? Can he leave all his friends forever? Find out where Fig's Heart belongs, and where he will call home, in this intriguing adventure.

Book 13 - Friday the 13th

Coral loses a tail feather and can't go to the carnival. See how Dew's family and friends try to help Coral get a replacement feather. And join them for the best Carnival of all!

And more stories are coming ...

Author's Note

I have so many people to thank, I would have to write a book of names. Add a splash of their personalities next to each name, and the book would be a comedy.

I have been blessed with a loving and supportive family (natural born and extended) and many truly awesome friends. I thank each and every one of you from the bottom of my heart.

We are all just moments in another person's time. Thank you all for being part of mine.

To learn more about Dew Bear or the author, please visit Dew's website at **www.dewbear.com** or e-mail your thoughts or questions to **dewbear@mindspring.com** or join us on facebook at www.facebook.com/Dew-Bear-Enterprises-Inc-1497926470453397/

DEBORAH DEEL CLAYTON was born in 1960 and grew up in Goffstown, New Hampshire. She now lives in Durham, North Carolina with her husband, Mike (Beezy), and has one awesome daughter, Denise Caron (Sharky).

"This third book in the Dew Bear series was inspired by my great-niece, Tessa. She truly is a fabulous and creative creature, overflowing with talents. She is a rare treasure that I am fortunate to have in my life."

"There are several important themes within this story. Some are easy to see—like that everyone has the ability to change if they really want to. Others are more subtle ... like not judging someone till you get to know them, sharing with others to make them happy, team-work, and just how wonderful making a wish can be (Make a Wish Foundation). But, the core ideals (ironically pronounced as "ahy-<u>deels</u>") live in all of Dew Bear's adventures—they are the value of friends and family, the importance of making memories, and the significance of love! Dew Bear's wish is that every life is filled to the honey pot brim with all three of these 'ahy-deels'!"

"Tessa really was having a 10th birthday when the original unpublished version of this story was written. However, due to the placement of this book as #3 in the series, Tessa had to wait 2 years for publication. August 3, 2016 is Tessa's 12th birthday and the official publication date."

HAPPY BIRTHDAY
TESSA